Shaky, Breaky School Sleuth

By J.L. Anderson

Illustrated by David Ouro

Rourke
Educational Media
rourkeeducationalmedia.com

www.rourkeeducationalmedia.com

Edited by: Keli Sipperley
Cover and Interior layout by: Jen Thomas
Cover and Interior Illustrations by: David Ouro

Library of Congress PCN Data

Shaky, Breaky School Sleuth / J.L. Anderson
 (Rourke's Mystery Chapter Books)
 ISBN (hard cover)(alk. paper) 978-1-63430-387-3
 ISBN (soft cover) 978-1-63430-487-0
 ISBN (e-Book) 978-1-63430-582-2
 Library of Congress Control Number: 2015933743

Printed in the United States of America,
North Mankato, Minnesota

Dear Parents and Teachers:

With twists and turns and red herrings, readers will enjoy the challenge of Rourke's Mystery Chapter Books. This series set at Watson Elementary School builds a cast of characters that readers quickly feel connected to. Embedded in each mystery are experiences that readers encounter at home or school. Topics of friendship, family, and growing up are featured within each book.

Mysteries open many doors for young readers and turn them into lifelong readers because they can't wait to find out what happens next. Readers build comprehension strategies by searching out clues through close reading in order to solve the mystery.

This genre spreads across many areas of study including history, science, and math. Exploring these topics through mysteries is a great way to engage readers in another area of interest. Reading mysteries relies on looking for patterns and decoding clues that help in learning math skills.

Whether readers are reading the books independently or you are reading with them, engaging with them after they have read the book is still important. We've included several activities at the end of each book to make this both fun and educational.

Do you think you and your reader have what it takes to be a detective? Can you solve the mystery? Will you accept the challenge?

Rourke Educational Media

Table of Contents

candy Dreams

Keely paused in front of the *Candy Dreams* school play sign-up sheet hanging outside of the music room. She held a pencil in her hand but she wasn't sure about auditioning. Keeping a secret was about the only thing she knew about acting.

"Did you forget your name or something?" Klaude asked, waiting for his turn to sign up. Of course a class clown like Klaude would want to be in the play. He loved being on stage. Keely rolled her eyes at him.

Keely's new friend, Queeneka, grabbed the pencil from Keely's hand. She signed up and added Keely's name under her own. "We're going to have a blast in the play together! I just know I'm going to get the part of Candy Princess. You'll get a good part too. I think." She muttered the last part under her breath.

Klaude signed up next and wrote his name above Queeneka's. "The lead part of the play will be Candy Prince, not Candy Princess."

"We'll have to see about that," Queeneka said. She turned around so fast her long braids almost whipped a boy named Javier in the face. He was next in line at the sign-up sheet.

When Queeneka didn't say a thing to Javier before walking off, Keely apologized for her. "Sorry, Queeneka's crazy about the play right now. I don't think she noticed you standing there."

"No big deal." Javier shrugged. He had pink paint smeared on the side of his nose. Javier was one of the best artists at Watson Elementary School. He'd been painting the set for Candy Dreams. His painting of cotton candy looked good enough for Keely to eat.

Keely watched as Javier held a pencil in his hand and paused for a moment, just as she'd done a few minutes before. Good thing Queeneka and Klaude already wrote their names on the list or they would've rushed him, too.

"You want to be in the play?" Keely asked. Not the best question, but she was surprised since Javier was shy and seemed more interested in painting the set than being in the play. That's how she felt, only she wasn't good at art. Keely didn't know what she was good at.

"Yeah, I do want to be in the play even if it will be hard for me," Javier said, still staring at the sign-up sheet as if it were a huge mountain he was about to climb. Then he wrote his name under Keely's.

That solved it. If Javier had it in him to try out for the school play, Keely could give it a try, too.

For the rest of the day, the third graders at Watson buzzed about *Candy Dreams*. "It would be cool if I got a part in the play to make my dad proud. He's coming home soon from the Army and maybe he can be there," a boy named Romy said.

"My costume for the lead part is going to be amazing," Queeneka said.

"Who cares about the costume? I'll put on the best show!" Klaude danced around the classroom and pretended to play a flute or something until Mr. Hambrick told him to knock it off.

Keely wasn't so excited. Whenever she got on the stage in music class, her knees buckled and words disappeared from her brain. She didn't want to get embarrassed in front of everyone at the audition. Javier must've been nervous too because his hands shook as he drew pictures of cats in outer space all over his notebook. Keely liked the one of a cat in a space suit orbiting Jupiter.

"Earth to Javier!" Mr. Hambrick said. The teacher spun around one of the planets hanging from the class ceiling. Javier looked up.

"I'm paying attention," Javier said and repeated the last couple of things Mr. Hambrick said in his lesson. Keely couldn't do that!

As soon as Mr. Hambrick went back to talking about the planets, Keely whispered to Javier, "Are you nervous?"

Just like she'd suspected, Javier nodded. "Only a little," he said. "I'll get a part no matter what."

Keely sighed. This was true. Whoever signed up for a part in the play would get to participate—even if the person's knees buckled and she couldn't remember what to say. The point of the audition was for Mrs. Tune to assign the character to the students. Keely could do this. Maybe.

The rest of the day seemed to drag on and then it was here. The audition!

Chapter Two

Keely's Audition
Nightmare

Mrs. Tune welcomed the group. "Thank you for trying out for *Candy Dreams*! Every one of you auditioning today will be given a role. No matter if it is a small part or the lead role, your performance together as a group will make this play a sweet success. We need help with the set crew as well, for those of you interested. Javier has done an amazing job painting scenes for the play."

The music room was full of kids and they all clapped for Javier. He sat close to Keely and she noticed his hands were shaking again as he waved to the group.

"I didn't know he was going to try out for the play," Queeneka whispered to Keely. "He's so quiet I wonder if anyone will hear him on stage."

Keely wasn't sure what to say since she worried about the same thing, only about herself. Would she be able to speak?

In the play, the Candy Prince or Princess goes missing in a crystal sugar cave, and pieces of candy must work together to find him or her trapped in a cotton candy blizzard. Mrs. Tune explained that everyone auditioning had to sing two short songs they'd learned in music class. She gave them the option of either singing in a small group or solo, if they felt comfortable. She passed out some *Candy Dreams* scripts, which each student would have to read from.

Just as Keely looked at the glowing exit sign above the music room door and thought of making a run for it, Mrs. Tune called her name to audition first. *What horrible luck*, she thought.

"Go break a leg, Keely," Queeneka said.

Keely nearly broke her leg as she tripped over Javier's notebook. "Sorry!" she said before she made her way up to the stage. Keely could barely breathe. Romy had asthma and Keely wondered if this is what he felt like when he had an attack.

"Would you like to sing a solo or sing in a

small group?" Mrs. Tune asked her.

The microphone looked like a weapon on the stage as Keely tried to speak into it. "Small group," Keely said, stretching her legs because her knees were starting to buckle.

"What was that, dear? You'll have to speak up," Mrs. Tune said.

"Small group," Keely repeated, but she had a feeling that her voice didn't come out any louder.

When Keely read from the first line of the script, her throat felt as though she'd swallowed a dozen cotton balls. Her eyes felt moist as she looked out at the audience. Some of the kids were laughing. Klaude probably was making fun of her.

Queeneka gave her a thumbs-up for encouragement and Javier smiled at her. She thought again how brave shy Javier was to audition. Keely was the type of girl who would rather blend into the background, but she secretly wanted to be bold like Queeneka. And she wanted to be brave like Javier. Keely took a deep breath and tried to be like both of them as she did what was right for her.

She set the script down and stepped away from the microphone. She looked at Mrs. Tune and said, "Thanks, but I'd rather be part of the set crew."

The microphone must've picked up her voice because the audience clapped. Maybe it was a pity clap or maybe the group was just happy her audition was over, Keely thought. She avoided making eye contact with anyone as she returned to her seat.

"Nice try," Queeneka said. "Now that I think about it, you're perfect for the set crew. At least now we don't have to fight about the lead role."

Keely laughed. That's all Queeneka could think about. And really, the girl was born to act. Keely stared at her friend in wonder when it was her turn to read from the lines and sing. She chose a solo and belted out a song about toffee troubles. Klaude didn't make a single joke when it was his turn. He danced polka moves while he sang about toffee. If Keely wasn't so impressed, she would've laughed.

Mrs. Tune would have a hard time choosing between the two of them, and four kids still hadn't auditioned, including Javier.

Keely watched as Javier's hands shook — especially the moment Mrs. Tune called his name. Javier took one look at the script, then set it aside before performing the lines. It was like he was painting, only it was in a different form.

Queeneka's jaw dropped open. Then she complained that it wasn't fair that he got to paint the set and be in the play. "Hold on a second—"

Queeneka started to say before Javier chose the solo song option.

Keely could see that Queeneka was trying to interrupt his performance. As much as she liked Queeneka, Keely wanted Javier to have a chance just like everyone else. "Shh," Keely said to Queeneka. "You had your turn already."

Javier––shy artist Javier!––sang the toffee song so well that it gave Keely the chills. Everyone clapped when he finished. Queeneka gave Keely a dirty look.

"Thank you all so much for trying out!" Mrs. Tune said at the end of the audition. "I'll post the cast list on Friday. Look for your name and the character you will play. I know some of you will be happy and some of you will be disappointed, but remember that we're all in this together. Please know that there won't be any changes to the list once it is made."

"If you get the part of the candy royalty, you'll regret it," Queeneka said to Javier.

Keely had already apologized for Queeneka once and she wasn't going to apologize again. She had a bad feeling about the play.

Chapter Three

practice makes problems

On Friday, Mrs. Tune posted the cast list outside of her door and a crowd gathered. Queeneka didn't wait for Keely as she elbowed her way to the front of the line.

Keely chose not to act in the play, but she was still curious to find out who got cast in what role. Word traveled down the line fast—Javier got the part of Candy Prince! Even though his audition had been great, the crowd gasped. Keely thought Queeneka might burst into tears, but she held her head up high.

Keely searched around for Javier to see his reaction and found him sitting on the music room floor cleaning up some paint. That was nice of him, Keely thought. She wondered if he knew the good news or not yet. Her attention turned

back to the line when Klaude got in Queeneka's face. "Told you that there was going to be a Candy Prince instead of a Candy Princess! I just wish I got the lead instead of Javier."

"Same here! Did you see the way Javier's hands shook at the audition? I bet he'll be too scared to act the night of the play," Queeneka said. "Whatever. Gum Drop is actually a better part than the prince or princess. I'll get more time on stage than the Candy Prince because he gets stuck in the cave."

"Well," Klaude said, "Licorice gets to dance plus sings a better solo than Gum Drop."

Romy cheered when he saw his part of Bubble Gum. "I don't care about any of that. I just hope my dad gets to see me!"

Some of the other kids whooped when they saw their parts. Others groaned. Keely watched as Queeneka walked into the music room and said something to Javier. He looked shocked. The next week of practice was going to be interesting, Keely thought.

******

The cast and the set crew rehearsed *Candy*

Dreams after school in the cafeteria. Keely discovered she really loved working on the set of a play. She was in charge of the music and she learned how to flip on some of the stage lights. Queeneka and Keely talked some, but not as much as before. Keely wondered if it still had to do with Javier or because they were both so busy with their schoolwork and their roles in the play.

Javier painted an amazing set with yummy looking candy pictures. In the middle of the play, Keely would have to go on stage and change out the pictures from summer – rainbow candy fruit – to winter – cotton candy storm pictures. Keely's favorite part of the set was a painting of the crystal cave the Candy Prince pretended to be trapped inside.

Mrs. Tune kept fussing at them all and pulling her hair. Just setting foot on the stage made it hard for Keely to breathe and she could barely move the set pieces. Javier did okay at practice, but not anywhere near as well as he had done in the audition. In fact, his hands shook even more.

Romy spoke out of turn and then had an

asthma attack. Klaude kept forgetting his lines, and Queeneka added lines to her character and made up a dance.

"I really want to impress Mrs. Holmes and your parents. Please don't let me down," Mrs. Tune said. Mrs. Holmes was the school principal.

"I'm not sure if I can pull my part off," Javier said after Mrs. Tune made him sing the same crystal sugar cave song three times. Mrs. Tune's hair stood up in every direction by the time he got it right.

Even if Mrs. Tune lost it some, the kids decided to get her a box of candy and a vase with some roses as a thank you gift for her hard work. Javier's parents were going to buy everything, and then they'd give her the gift at the end of the play the following night.

For now, Javier sat off in the corner of the cafeteria during a short break. "You okay?' Keely asked him, even though she knew he wasn't okay.

"Acting in the play was a bad idea," he said.

"Are you kidding? You're so talented it isn't even fair," Keely said.

Mrs. Tune clapped her hands for them to get back to work. Javier's performance got worse as the practice session continued. Other kids struggled too and Keely had to give a couple more pep talks. That seemed to be another job of set crew. Klaude sat on the ground, pouting while he tinkered with a wooden instrument.

"I don't know if I'll remember my lines tomorrow," Klaude confessed to Keely.

Keely noticed that he'd been learning Licorice's lines as well as the Candy Prince's lines. "If you just focus on your part and not on Javier's then it will be easier."

"Yeah," Klaude said, "I plan on playing his part too since I think he's going to change his mind."

Keely hoped that didn't happen.

"I should've been the Candy Princess," Queeneka told Keely as they waited for their parents to pick them up.

"Yeah, but no one would play the part of Gum Drop as well as you," Keely said.

Queeneka smiled at that. "Sorry if I was rude before. I just want this so badly, you know?"

Keely didn't know exactly, but she gave Queeneka a hug. She wanted to be friends again.

That night Keely had a hard time sleeping because she was thinking about the play and all the things that could go wrong. She had no idea what was in store.

Chapter Four

Javier is Missing

Keely wore a cotton-candy pink shirt and a matching tutu the night of the play. She felt fancy and would blend in on the stage when she changed the set. Keely's parents changed out of their usual Scoop Troop business shirts and wore nice dress pants and button-down shirts. "We're so proud of you, Keely," they said.

When Keely went behind the curtain on the cafeteria stage before the play started, she was surprised to see Mrs. Tune's hair wilder than ever. "I don't know what we're going to do," Mrs. Tune said, pacing back and forth.

"What's going on?" Keely asked Queeneka. Queeneka was playing the part of Gum Drop, but she looked just like a princess with her braids twisted into a crown on top of her head.

"Javier is missing!" Queeneka said. She led

Keely to the side of the room where Javier set his costume. It was folded neatly on top of a chair. Shattered glass sprinkled the floor like dangerous shards of hard candy. The roses lay scattered about and Romy almost slipped in the water. "I think he's been kidnapped."

"No way," Klaude said, then walked over to Mrs. Tune. "Don't worry. I'll be able to play Javier's part. I've been practicing."

"That's nice of you to help, Klaude, but I'm not so sure about your plan. More importantly, how am I going to explain to Mrs. Holmes that my lead actor is missing? If he doesn't show up soon, I must call the police."

"Javier wasn't sure if he was going to pull his part off. He probably ran off home so he wouldn't be embarrassed in front of everyone," Romy said.

That was something Keely would've wanted to do, but she wasn't so sure Javier was the type to run off. Like Keely, Javier had to ride the school bus because it was too far and dangerous to walk home. Besides, his family was already here, waiting for their star to go onstage.

"Why would he have smashed the vase?" Keely asked.

"I've been so hard on him," Mrs. Tune said. She had tears in her eyes.

Keely volunteered to help. "I'll check with Javier's family and ask Mr. Sleuth if Javier has a number to call at home."

Mrs. Tune rubbed her temples before pulling at her hair again. Mr. Sleuth was the school secretary, and he could be really nosy. "I won't say why," Keely added. Mrs. Tune was worried enough as it was. "I know we're going to find Javier and he'll be perfectly fine."

"I should talk to the audience and cancel the

play," Mrs. Tune said. Her hair was hedgehog-spiky looking now.

Keely was part of the set crew, but she had a more important mission now. "Give me at least 15 minutes to find Javier after I talk to Mr. Sleuth."

"I can stall the audience with a dance or two," Klaude said. "My grandma is here and she can help, too. She used to be a professional dancer."

"I can sing some songs," Queeneka said. A few other kids promised they'd help stall the show for as long as they could.

"I'll do what I can, but has anyone seen my dad?" Romy asked. No one had.

The crowd looked anxious and bored as Keely searched for Javier's family. His dad looked like a penguin in his suit and Javier's mom matched him in a black and white dress. Javier's two little brothers wore matching penguin suits.

"I'm Javier's friend," Keely said as she talked to his parents. "Have you seen him in the past couple minutes?"

"Not since we dropped him off," Javier's mom said. "I wanted to take lots of behind the scene pictures, but he told me that it was bad luck and promised to take photos later. Is everything okay?"

How was Keely supposed to answer that? Javier was missing and she didn't want to worry his family yet. "I, uh, uh, just wanted to get his autograph."

Javier's dad smiled wide when she said that.

"I'll guess I have to wait until later like the pictures," Keely said.

Keely and Javier's family looked up as Mrs. Tune came out on stage to make an announcement. She must've brushed her hair to look less frazzled. "We've had a delay, and if all goes well, the play will start shortly. But first, we have a small talent show for your entertainment."

The crowd clapped as Queeneka stepped out on stage and burst into song. Keely had to hurry. Time was running out!

keely Looks for clues

As Keely searched for Mr. Sleuth, she thought through the events. Klaude had practiced for Javier's part. It was like he expected Javier to disappear. Had he done something to Javier?

And Queeneka wanted the lead role just as much as Klaude. She'd tried to mess up his audition and said something to Javier in the music room—was it a threat of some kind? Javier had looked shocked when she said it. And what was up with Queeneka's comment that Javier would regret it if he got the part of the Candy Prince? Was Queeneka warning Javier that she would do something to him?

Keely was friends with Queeneka and didn't want to think she was capable of sabotaging

Javier's big night, but the play had already brought out the worst in her.

What if Klaude and Queeneka had joined forces to do something to Javier? Keely hoped that was impossible, but given the way the two of them were so crazy about the play and being the center of attention, she didn't know anymore. What would they have done to him, though? Keely gulped. Klaude and Queeneka surely weren't capable of hurting Javier.

Or were they?

Keely found Mr. Sleuth by the front of the cafeteria door greeting some of the parents who straggled in late to the play. Mrs. Holmes stood on the other side of the door and handed the parents programs, then glanced up at the stage to see the talent show unfolding. Keely could tell by Mrs. Holmes's eyes that she was concerned.

Keely needed to be tricky so she wouldn't raise any alarms. "Can I ask for your help, Mr. Sleuth?"

The school secretary smiled. "Of course! Anything for one of the best set crew workers Watson has ever seen."

Keely must've looked as surprised as she felt inside because Mr. Sleuth said, "Mrs. Tune said so."

Keely needed to focus on finding Javier, but she couldn't help herself. "Really?"

"Really! Now what can I do for you? Something to help get the play started?" Mr. Sleuth asked.

He has no idea, she thought. "Can you make a quick phone call for me? Javier—" Keely started to whisper but she didn't want to tell a lie. "Well, he might've gone home. Maybe he left to pick something up that he forgot?"

"I'll be back in a moment," Mr. Sleuth said to Mrs. Holmes. Good thing the principal was busy talking to Romy's mom or else she might've asked some questions.

Mr. Sleuth led Keely to the office. It looked strange to see the office at night, dark and without all of the teachers and the students everywhere.

This would be a good spot to hide a lead actor if you wanted to take his spot, Keely thought. She walked around while Mr. Sleuth called

Javier's home line, listening in closely to the locked doors. She jumped when she heard a *clunk, clunk* by the teacher's workroom.

Had she found Javier?

Keely nearly screamed as a shadow towered over her while she pressed her ear against the door.

It was Mr. Sleuth. "Javier didn't answer. Is everything all right?"

Just then there was another *clunk, clunk*!

"Is someone or something locked in there?" Keely asked.

Mr. Sleuth laughed. "That's just the ice machine. Other than you kids, it's the noisiest thing in all of Watson."

"I see," Keely said.

"Ha! Good pun—icy!" Mr. Sleuth said.

Keely shook her head. She wasn't trying to make a pun—she had a case to solve and Mrs. Tune was minutes away from canceling the play.

"Thanks, Mr. Sleuth, and see you later!" Keely said, racing off to rejoin the cast. Maybe Javier would be there, dressed and ready to put on the play.

As Keely was about to go behind the curtain, she nearly bumped into a short man in a uniform. He turned around and hid himself behind a display in the first grade hall.

How strange, Keely thought.

Chapter Six

Foul Play?

No luck. Javier was still missing when Keely rejoined the cast of *Candy Dreams*.

"Did you get ahold of Javier?" Mrs. Tune asked. She needed to brush her hair again.

Keely shook her head. "No one answered the phone."

"Maybe he refused to answer it," Romy said. Klaude was stretching before his dance performance. Queeneka was wrapping up her second song.

"Doubt it," Keely said. She moved close to Klaude so she could talk to him privately. "I know how much you wanted the part of Candy Prince. Did you pull some kind of joke on Javier so he'd be late?"

Klaude's eyes grew wide. "Sure I wanted the part, but he got cast as the prince fair and square.

My audition was good, but his was better."

"Why were you studying for his part then? You seemed to expect something like this to happen," Keely said right as the audience clapped for Queeneka.

"We all saw Javier struggling. You heard him say that he wasn't sure if he could pull it off with your own ears. I didn't want the play to get canceled in case Javier changed his mind. It might get canceled any way if Javier doesn't show."

Keely's gut instinct told her that Klaude was telling the truth. That left Queeneka as the main suspect.

Queeneka was glowing as she joined the cast behind the curtain. "Well done," Mrs. Tune managed to say. "This evening won't be a complete disaster." She went back to searching for Javier along with a few others as Klaude went out on stage next.

"Come on up, Oma!" Keely heard Klaude say into the microphone.

Keely didn't have the time to tiptoe around Queeneka's feelings. "Did you do something to in the music room! And I figured he'd regret getting the lead because he's shy and gets so nervous. Have you forgotten the way his hands shake? I was practicing with Romy when he went missing."

Keely walked up to Romy while Queeneka followed. She had to be sure Queeneka wasn't lying. "Romy, were you practicing with anyone earlier?"

"Queeneka," Romy said, wheezing. Keely hoped he wouldn't have another asthma attack.

"Some friend you are, Keely! I can't believe you thought I might've kidnapped him or trapped him in some sort of crystal cave."

Keely shrugged, unable to speak because something was bothering her. At least Queeneka seemed innocent. This was a huge relief to Keely and she'd find a way to make it up to her friend later. For now, Queeneka had to settle for a quick apology. "Sorry."

The audience in the cafeteria laughed. Klaude must have been doing a good job entertaining everyone with his grandmother. Keely hoped he could keep it up so she could find Javier.

Sure he was shy and acted nervous a lot, but Keely doubted he'd gone home or run away.

Klaude seemed innocent of foul play. *Foul play – Mr. Sleuth would've liked that pun,* Keely thought, and then made herself focus.

None of the other kids in the play seemed like they had motive to kidnap or sabotage Javier. So what about Mrs. Tune? She'd admitted to being hard on Javier. Maybe she did something to him so he wouldn't mess up her precious play. But would she have broken her own flower vase? Not to mention that Mrs. Tune was about to call the police she was so worried about Javier.

Keely returned to the thought that bothered her—the man in the uniform who was acting so strange by the cafeteria. Was he a kidnapper?

Had he smashed the vase when he took Javier hostage?

"I need your help, Queeneka," Keely said, grabbing her hand. Mrs. Tune talked about working together as a team for the play, and Keely needed a teammate now more than ever. If the man was dangerous, she didn't want to be alone when she confronted him. Queeneka could probably scream as loud as she could sing and they'd be safer together.

"What are you doing?" Queeneka asked as Keely led her down the first grade hall.

Keely didn't have time to explain. She searched for the man in the uniform and found him lurking by the display. As soon as he saw the girls walking, he turned around and took off.

"You stop right there!" Keely yelled.

Chapter Seven

Finding the crystal cave

The man in the uniform stopped and turned back around.

"Are you a kidnapper?" Keely asked him. Queeneka jumped back in surprise.

Again, it wasn't the best question. Who would admit to being a kidnapper if he was actually a kidnaper? Keely asked another question before the man in the uniform had time to answer the first one. "What have you done with Javier?"

The man raised his arms up as if to prove his innocence. "I don't know what you're talking about. I'm here to see my son."

"Then why are you hiding in the hallway?" Keely asked, still suspicious that the man might've done something. "All of the parents are waiting in the cafeteria to see their kids."

The man lowered his arms and that's when she noticed that the name *Ramirez* was stitched on the man's Army uniform. Ramirez was Romy's last name. Hadn't Romy been hoping all along that his dad would show up at the play?

Queeneka must've been figuring things out too because she said, "Are you Romy's dad?"

"Yes." The man smiled. "I've been gone overseas for a while and just returned home. Mrs. Holmes said it would be okay if I surprised Romy. I avoided you because I didn't want anyone to see me to give the surprise away. I was supposed to come out at the beginning of the play, but there's been some kind of delay."

"The delay is because we're missing the lead actor, Javier," Keely said. "I'm doing everything I can to find him so the play won't get canceled."

"I'll keep my eyes open for any suspicious activity," Romy's dad said. "I sure hope the play doesn't get canceled."

Keely had even more reason to find Javier now. She and Queeneka walked down the hallway back to the cafeteria, deep in thought.

"You don't think I'm guilty anymore, do you?"

Queeneka asked after a moment.

"No. I'm sorry if I hurt your feelings," Keely said.

"I can see why you thought I might've done something, given the clues," Queeneka said. "I really am sorry for being obsessed about the play. Javier has to be around here somewhere, don't you think?"

Keely paused to see if she could hear any cries for help. Then her mind returned to the clues. She thought about the busted vase. Maybe it hadn't broken in some sort of struggle.

Maybe it broke because of an accident.

"Shaky hands!" Keely cried.

"You're losing it, Keely," Queeneka said.

"No, hear me out. I think Javier dropped the vase on accident. You reminded me about his shaky hand syndrome earlier," Keely said.

"Okay, I think it is likely he dropped the vase, but where is he?"

Keely remembered the way Javier had cleaned the paint off of the music room floor when he could've been in line to find out the casting announcement. If he broke the vase on

47

accident, he probably felt bad about it and didn't want to leave the mess for anyone else to clean up.

Keely had an idea!

"Follow me, Queeneka. And hurry!" Keely wasn't acting in *Candy Dreams*, but she felt like she was one of the candies searching for the crystal cave.

******

"Why are you girls not in the play?" the custodian asked when Keely and Queeneka walked into the school's basement.

"We're looking for our friend Javier," Keely said. "He's the star of the play. Have you seen him?"

The custodian shook his head. "The play is taking place in the cafeteria, not in the basement."

"It's kind of scary down here," Queeneka said looking around.

Keely heard a strange noise, kind of like a ghost would make in a movie. "It's not haunted is it?"

The custodian shook his head again. "No,

but it seems that way tonight. My mop must've fallen over and I think something fell off a shelf earlier."

"Javier!" Keely and Queeneka yelled at the same time.

standing ovations

The custodian unlocked the supply closet door and Javier practically fell out of the small room. Keely was right!

"The supply door was wide open," the custodian said. "I never thought to look for a student inside before I locked it up."

The custodian started to say something else, but Javier cut him off. "Did I miss the play?" he asked.

"There's a chance we can still make it," Keely said. "Are you okay? Can you run?"

"Yes!" Javier said, taking off before Keely and Queeneka had a chance.

The dash to the cafeteria seemed to take a long time and Keely giggled because it was crazy running down the hall in her cotton candy pink tutu with Queeneka and Javier. She was

overjoyed that they'd found him and that he was okay.

When they got to the back of the stage in the cafeteria, the whole cast of *Candy Dreams* –minus Romy – greeted Javier. Romy was onstage with his little brother doing a hand clapping routine.

Mrs. Tune hugged Javier. "What happened to you?"

"I was like the Candy Prince only I got locked in the supply closet instead. I'll explain more later. Is the play still on?" Javier asked.

"Do you think you can still play the part of the Candy Prince?" Mrs. Tune asked.

"Yes! I understand the prince better now." Javier held up his hands. Keely was surprised— they were steady. Maybe it was from the solitude of being locked in the closet or maybe he got his nerves out by running in the hall. "I just need a moment to get ready."

"I'm afraid we don't have moments to spare. The audience is restless and so is Mrs. Holmes," Mrs. Tune said.

"I can help," Keely said, regretting the words

the moment they came out of her mouth.

"How?" Klaude asked. "What talent are you going to share?"

"I may not be able to sing or dance or act, but I love to help people," Keely said. "That has to count for something."

"It does! Keely and Queeneka saved me from the custodian's closet," Javier said as he shoved his costume over his clothes.

"That was all Keely," Queeneka said, patting Keely on the back.

Keely's face felt hot as the whole cast and set crew stared at her. Or maybe her face felt hot because of what she was about to do.

The moment Keely stepped out on stage, the lights blinded her. The audience clapped for Romy and his little brother and the roar of the noise felt like nothing compared to the pounding in her heart as she walked over to the microphone. It looked dangerous to her.

As Romy and his little brother were about to exit the stage to give Keely a turn, she called out, "Wait!" Her voice actually came out in a boom.

Romy and his little brother looked at Keely as

if she had lost her mind. She supposed she had. Maybe the run and all of her detective work had done something to calm down her nerves too.

"Thank you all for coming to the play tonight," Keely said. If she didn't stop to think about it and looked right at her parents, it was easier to talk. "This is a special night for all of us and it is an extra special night for some." She didn't have to say much more because Mr. Ramirez, Romy's dad, made his way onto the stage, hugging his sons.

"Welcome home!" Keely said to Romy's dad. Romy and his brother jumped into their dad's arms. The audience gave a standing ovation. Keely noticed Mrs. Holmes dabbing tears from her eyes.

As Mrs. Tune thanked the audience again for their patience, Queeneka leaned into Keely. "You were amazing. Maybe you should try out for the school play next year."

"I plan to sign up for set crew again," Keely said.

The play began without any issues and the students did an amazing job. Javier's performance was even better than his audition. Klaude remembered his lines and Queeneka didn't add too many extra ones. The cast and crew of *Candy Dreams* got a standing ovation at the end, too.

The custodian felt so bad about Javier getting locked in the closet that he found a pretty cup from the basement to put the roses in after he cleaned up the mess. Keely thought Mrs. Tune was going to cry again when the cast handed her the messy bouquet at the end of the play.

"I hope you all feel proud of yourselves," Mrs. Tune said to the cast.

Keely had never been more proud!

.

How to Solve a Mystery, By Keely

I had no idea a play would have so many mysteries to solve! The first mystery of course was who would be cast for each part. But the biggest mystery was when Javier disappeared. To solve that one, I first had to figure out if he made himself disappear.

Because Javier was shy, everyone seemed to think that Javier ran off. To check for myself, I had Mr. Sleuth call Javier's home, but that didn't give me any leads. I trusted in my gut that he didn't run away.

Next I thought about who would have a motive to keep Javier from performing in the play. Klaude and Queeneka were suspects because they wanted Javier's part. To get some answers, I had to interview them both. To decide if a suspect is telling the truth, a detective checks their alibis, or the people they were with when the suspicious activity took place.

When they checked out, I thought through other possibilities. There was one clue—the broken vase. A good detective puts everything she knows together to reconstruct the scene. Thinking about the clue along with the type of person Javier is led me to the answer!

Red Herrings

Red herrings are false clues that writers sprinkle throughout mystery stories. Red herrings are fun to include as a writer because they can lead readers to suspect the wrong characters or get the wrong idea about the mystery. These false clues make the mystery more challenging to figure out and can make the story more interesting. Writers can then slip in the real clues without making them obvious to the readers.

When writing red herrings, it is important to make sure that they make sense in the story. For example, Romy's dad was a red herring—he seemed suspicious hanging out in the hallway. His behavior made sense because he wanted to surprise Romy, and Romy had shared how much he was hoping his father could be there earlier in the story.

Discussion Questions

1. What part in the play would you have wanted and why?
2. Have you ever not been picked for a role or a position on a team you wanted? How did you respond to the disappointment?
3. Who did you identify with in the story the most and why?
4. Which character did you suspect was guilty and for what reasons?
5. Do any of the characters remind you of people you know? How so?

Vocabulary

Play a game of charades! Take turns acting out each of these vocabulary words with a friend.

apologize: say sorry
audition: tryout
doubted: felt uncertain
frazzled: worn out
lurking: creep around
ovation: long applause
overjoyed: really happy
participate: take part
performance: act, show
sabotage: damage on purpose
shattered: broken
suspicious: untrustworthy
tutu: skirt worn as a costume
volunteered: offered, help

Writing Prompt

1. Rewrite this mystery and have Queeneka, Klaude, or Mrs. Tune hide Javier on purpose.
2. Write a story based on the play scene—what if one of the other characters go missing or some other mystery occurs as the play unfolds in front of the school audience? Try to include drama, suspense, and humor.
3. Write a mystery based on the school play, *Candy Dreams*. How does the Candy Princess or Prince get taken and how do the candy characters find the crystal cave to save the princess or prince?

Websites to Visit

Play some detective games:
www.fbi.gov/fun-games/kids/kids-games

Learn how to overcome stage fright:
www.speaking-tips.com/Stage-Fright

Practice your acting skills with drama games:
www.bbbpress.com/dramagames

About the Author

J. L. Anderson solves a mystery of her own almost every day like figuring out why her daughter is suddenly so quiet (what did she get into this time?), which of her two dogs stole the bag of treats, where her husband is taking her for a surprise dinner, or what happened to her keys this time. You can learn more about J.L. Anderson at www.jessicaleeanderson.com.

About the Illustrator

I have always loved drawing from a very young age. While I was at school, most of my time was spent drawing comics and copying my favorite characters. With a portfolio under my arm, I started drawing comics for newspapers and fanzines. After I finished my studies I decided to try to make a living as a freelance illustrator... and here I am!